W9-BAA-195

The ELVES and the SHOEMAKER

WITHDRAWN

The **ELVES** and the

SHOEMAKER

A FOLK TALE CLASSIC

Retold and Illustrated by

PAUL GALDONE

Based on Lucy Crane's translation
from the German of the Brothers Grimm

HOUGHTON MIFFLIN HARCOURT
Boston   New York

COVINGTON BRANCH LIBRARY
NEWTON COUNTY LIBRARY SYSTEM
7116 FLOYD STREET
COVINGTON, GA 30014

To Americo Loiola, master shoemaker,
and family

Copyright © 1984 by The Estate of Paul Galdone

All rights reserved. Originally published in hardcover in the United States by Clarion
Books, an imprint of Houghton Mifflin Harcourt Publishing Company, 1984.

For information about permission to reproduce selections from this book,
write to trade.permissions@hmhco.com or to Permissions, Houghton Mifflin Harcourt
Publishing Company, 3 Park Avenue, 19th Floor, New York, New York 10016.

www.hmhco.com

The Library of Congress Cataloging-in-Publication data is on file.

ISBN: 978-0-544-53099-7

Manufactured in China
SCP 10 9 8 7 6 5 4 3 2

4500710655

There once was a shoemaker who, through no fault of his own, became so poor that at last he had nothing left but just enough leather to make one pair of shoes. He cut out the shoes at night, so he could set to work on them the next morning.

Because he had a good conscience, the shoemaker laid
himself down in his bed and fell asleep at once.

In the morning, after he had said his prayers, the shoemaker went to his workshop. There he found the pair of shoes made and finished, and standing on his table. He was very much astonished, and could not tell what to think.

He took the shoes in his hand to examine them more carefully. They were so well made that every stitch was in the right place, just as if they had come from the hand of a master-workman.

Soon a customer entered, and as the shoes fitted
him very well, he paid more than the usual price
for them.

Now the shoemaker had enough money to buy
leather for two more pairs of shoes. He cut them out
at night and intended to set to work the next morning
with fresh spirit. But that was not to be, for when he
got up they were already finished.

A customer soon bought them and gave the shoemaker
so much money that he was able to buy enough leather
for four more pairs.

Early the next morning he found the four pairs finished also. And so it always happened. Whatever the shoemaker cut out in the evening was finished by the morning, and soon he was making a very good living.

One night, not long before Christmas, when the shoemaker had finished cutting out the shoes from the leather, he turned to his wife before he went to bed and said: "How would it be if we were to stay up tonight and see who it is that does us this service?"

His wife agreed, and set a candle to burn.
Then they both hid in a corner of the room,
behind some coats that were hanging up. They
peeked out between the coats and began
to watch.

As soon as it was midnight, in came two neatly formed naked little elves. They seated themselves on the shoemaker's table, took up the work that was already prepared,

and began to stitch, pierce, and hammer the leather.
The elves worked so cleverly and quickly with their
little fingers that the shoemaker's eyes could
scarcely follow them, so full of wonder was he.

The elves never stopped until all the shoes were
finished and were standing ready on the table.
Then they jumped up and ran off.

The next morning the shoemaker's wife said to
her husband, "Those elves have made us rich,
and we ought to show them how grateful we are.

With all their running about, and nothing to cover them, they must be very cold."

She smiled. "I tell you what. I will make little shirts, coats, waistcoats, and breeches for them, and knit each of them a pair of stockings. And you shall make each of them a pair of shoes!"

The husband consented willingly, and that night,
when everything was finished,
they laid the gifts on the table
instead of the cut-out leather.

Then they hid themselves so that they could observe
how the elves behaved when they saw their presents.

At the stroke of midnight the elves rushed in,
ready to set to work. But when they found
the neat little clothes made just for them
they stood a moment in surprise, and then
they showed the greatest delight.

Quickly they took up the pretty garments and
slipped them on, singing,

> *What spruce and dandy boys are we!*
> *No longer cobblers will we be.*

They hopped and danced about, jumping over the chairs and tables, and at last they danced out the door.

From that time on the elves were never seen again.
But the shoemaker and his wife prospered as long
as they lived.

AUG 2 7 2019